by S. Prue

illustrated by Steve May

Librarian Reviewer
Kathleen Baxter
Children's Literature Consultant
formerly with Anoka County Library, MN
BA College of Saint Catherine, St. Paul, MN
MA in Library Science, University of Minnesota

Reading Consultant
Elizabeth Stedem
Educator/Consultant, Colorado Springs, CO
MA in Elementary Education, University of Denver, CO

▼▼ STONE ARCH BOOKS
Minneapolis   San Diego

First published in the United States in 2007
by Stone Arch Books,
151 Good Counsel Drive, P.O. Box 669,
Mankato, Minnesota 56002.
www.stonearchbooks.com

Originally published in Great Britain in 2005
by A & C Black Publishers Ltd,
38 Soho Square, London, W1D 3HB.

Library of Congress Cataloging-in-Publication Data
Prue, Sally.
    James and the Alien Experiment / by S. Prue; illustrated by Steve May.
    p. cm. — (Pathway Books)
    Summary: When James is abducted by aliens, he undergoes some
drastic changes, but although his super powers make him the most popular
boy at school, they cause him more problems than he had bargained for.
    ISBN-13: 978-1-59889-111-9 (hardcover)
    ISBN-10: 1-59889-111-1 (hardcover)
    ISBN-13: 978-1-59889-260-4 (paperback)
    ISBN-10: 1-59889-260-6 (paperback)
    [1. Extraterrestrial beings—Fiction. 2. Schools—Fiction.] I. May,
Steve, ill. II. Title. III. Series.
PZ7.P9493492Jam 2007
[Fic]—dc22   2006005082

Art Director: Heather Kindseth
Graphic Designer: Kay Fraser

1 2 3 4 5 6 11 10 09 08 07 06

Printed in the United States of America.

Table of Contents

Chapter 1

One afternoon, James Hunter was kidnapped by aliens.

He was just sitting in his living room when the TV started making weird noises. Then some writing appeared on the screen. It said:

> YOU ARE ABOUT TO BE KIDNAPPED BY ALIENS. PLEASE DO NOT ADJUST YOUR TV

The screen turned a shining green with swirls. Then the swirls came together, until it looked as if a bony hand was reaching out of the set.

Another commercial, thought James. Boring. He sighed.

It did look real, though. It was a really good special effect. If the program was any good, though, if it was really scary, then it would be on after bedtime and he wouldn't be allowed to watch it.

Some more writing came up on the screen. It said:

```
    WE APOLOGIZE FOR
  ANY INCONVENIENCE
```

And then the bony hand zoomed right out of the screen and grabbed him.

James couldn't believe it. Huge fingers had clamped themselves around his waist. As he stared down, frozen in horror, they lifted him out of his chair. "Hey!" he said. "What do you think you're doing? Let me go!"

James put up his arm to protect his head from the glass of the television screen, but the glass seemed to have vanished. He saw wires as he was pulled right into the TV.

He pulled, but the bony hand was as hard as rock and he couldn't get away.

James was going so fast, and he had no idea where he was going.

At first everything was blurry, but after a few seconds he saw squares of blue and gray, and then, far below him, a green rectangle. That was the football stadium on the other side of town.

Then something wet hit him right in the face. He wiped his eyes, and saw that there was a cloud underneath him, shining like a golden cauliflower.

I'm being kidnapped by aliens, he thought. He was too amazed to take it in.

There was something in the sky in front of him. It was a building, or maybe a spaceship, and it was glowing like flames. I'm being kidnapped by aliens, he thought again. This time he believed it.

He closed his eyes, opened his mouth, and he screamed.

* * *

James was lying on something cold, and all around him were the ticking and purring sounds of machinery. "Yuck," said a voice nearby. "It's gross."

James kept his eyes squeezed shut and hoped very hard that he was dreaming.

"It looks dead to me," said another, deeper voice.

I'm asleep, thought James, trying to believe it. I'm asleep.

Ow!

He opened his eyes because something was poking him. There was a thing right in front of him. It was all green and slimy, and it had purple eyes and a small trunk. James screamed again.

"Ah," said the thing, blinking at him and looking pleased. "Good. Not dead, after all. Let's get down to business."

There were two of them. The one over at the control panel, who had six-inch eyelashes and sparkles on its antenna, pressed a gleaming silver button.

"Let me go!" said James. "Let me go! I want to go home!"

The nearest alien said, "Don't be silly. This is your lucky day."

James scrambled to his feet.

"No, it's not!" he said. "What do you want with me?"

"All sorts of things," said the nearest alien. "I am Improver Pockle of the planet Terkle, and this is Assistant Improver Trada. We're going to redesign you."

Chapter 2

"I don't know why you're screaming," said Pockle. "We give up our time to fly around the universe helping all you aliens, and you don't care. Don't you understand that we're trying to do you a favor?"

"Yeah," said Trada. She was painting her ear lobes a shiny blue. "I mean, you're so ugly. No antenne. No slime. I mean, yuck!"

"Yes," said Pockle. "Now, what would you like us to do? We could change your legs into wheels."

He smiled.

"Or we could give you arms you can dig with," he added. "Think how nice that would be. If you wanted an extra room in your house, you could dig yourself one in no time at all."

"I want to go home!" said James.

Pockle waddled over to a stool and lifted himself onto it.

"A tail?" he suggested. "Mine is very useful. It keeps me cool, and it's ideal for swatting bats. Or how about sharper teeth to help with eating?"

James shuddered. "I have to go home," he said. "My mom will be worried."

"Oh, there's no need to worry about your mother," Pockle said. He shook his head. "This ship is going almost as fast as time, so that means you've only been gone a couple of seconds."

"Now, how about flying?" asked the alien. "That's always popular. Think of playing fighter pilots. Think of being able to drop stink bombs down people's chimneys and then watch them come out all green in the face and blaming each other."

James hesitated. That did sound fun. "If I could fly I'd be just like Superman," he said.

"That's right."

Pockle rubbed his paws together. "We'll add one thing each day, so we can monitor exactly what effect it has, but you can have any superpower you like. Super smell, perhaps?"

James Hunter, Superboy?

James thought that was such a great idea that his brain almost exploded.

What superpower should he choose? Not super smell, or bad smells would be even worse.

Something on one of the control panels began to beep. Trada put down her bottle of ear-lobe paint and looked at the display.

"Something's flashing," she reported. "The thing with pointers."

"Ah. The clock, you mean," said Pockle.

"Yeah, that's right, I remember now. It's for telling the time. That buzzer thing means that if we don't hurry up, we won't be able to send him back today."

James thought about his choices. Being able to fly would be awesome.

X-ray vision would be really neat too. With x-ray vision he'd be able to find the best baseball card packs before he paid for them.

"Countdown," announced Trada. "Nine minutes and fifty-five seconds. Nine minutes and fifty seconds. Nine minutes and forty-five seconds."

James was trying to decide, but his brain was so full of ideas that he just couldn't.

"You'll have to hurry," said Pockle. "We could make you a nicer color, if you like. Green, maybe."

James shook his head. He couldn't decide. He liked to think about things carefully. He wished he were quicker.

Yeah! That was what he'd have. That would be great. Finally he made his decision. James felt a huge grin spreading over his face at the thought.

"Super speed," he said. "That's what I want. I want to be the fastest person in the entire world."

Trada pressed buttons. "You'll fall asleep for a while," Pockle told James, "and when you wake up you'll be back home. You might even think this has all been a dream, until your incredible super speed starts working tomorrow morning."

"How fast am I going to be?" asked James, his heart pounding.

"Oh, really fast. Faster than anyone's ever been. Ready?"

"But what if something goes wrong?" James asked. He felt nervous and excited.

Pockle smiled. "Don't worry, we'll bring you back up here tomorrow night for a checkup, and then if anything's not working we can fix it, or even take it away. Everything ready, Miss Trada?"

"Well, I plugged in the thingy," Trada said, chewing her gum.

"Here goes!" said Pockle.

At that moment, James suddenly realized what was going to happen. Aliens were about to start messing around with his body. He opened his mouth to tell them to stop, but Pockle was pulling down a big handle on the control panel. It was too late.

James saw huge, colorful explosions. Then everything went black.

 Chapter 3

What a dream! thought James. He looked at the TV. The news was on, so he must have slept through his cartoon.

"Oh good, you're awake," said Mom. "I thought I was going to have to carry you up to bed."

James sat up. "My arms and legs feel like they have worms wiggling around inside them," he said.

"They just fell asleep because of the way you've been lying," said Mom.

James shook his head. His skin felt weird and parts of him twitched.

I must still be half-asleep, he thought.

He went to bed.

* * *

James woke up the next morning from a deep sleep to hear Mom pounding on his bedroom door.

"James! Are you awake?"

James groaned.

"Rise and shine!" called Mom.

James didn't want to get up. He had horrible dreams about worms all night. He just wanted to lie there and be glad they were gone.

"James!" called Mom again.

"Coming," he said, lying in bed.

The door handle suddenly turned and his bossy big sister, Tina, poked her head around the door.

She looked mad and mean, but that was mostly because of her purple hair, inch-long fake nails, and the tattoo on her neck.

"Mom!" she called down the stairs. "He's still in bed!"

James leaped out of bed. He pulled off his pajamas and jumped into his clothes. Then he brushed his hair. He made his bed and put his dirty clothes in his laundry bag. All in less than one minute.

James stood in his tidy room and breathed. He couldn't believe it. All that stuff about the aliens was real, and it had really worked. He, James Hunter, was the fastest person on Earth.

When Mom came in, she found James dressed and ready.

"Oh!" she said. "Tina said you were still in bed."

"I was just resting," said James. "It was very tiring cleaning my room."

Mom laughed and told him to hurry up and come down to breakfast. She paused in the doorway.

"Something smells in here," she said.

James couldn't smell anything.

"Like something burning," she said. "You haven't been playing with matches, have you?"

"No," said James. He hadn't.

Mom shrugged. "Weird," she said. "I'll have to check your electric blanket."

James ate all his eggs and bacon, and then he had seven slices of toast.

"You're disgusting," said Tina, biting into her fourth piece of toast.

"No time for more," said Mom. "You'll be late for school."

James ate some more toast and a cookie before he got up from the table. He could never remember feeling so hungry in his life.

He left for school three minutes before nine. Mom was freaking out by then.

"You'll be late," she said, for the twelfth time, "and then you'll be in trouble with Mrs. Sharply. Hurry up!"

His previous record for running to school was five and a half minutes, but that day James did it in under thirty seconds.

Mom was right. He did smell something burning. It was so strong when he got to school that James was hoping the school burned down in the night. When he turned the corner, the school wasn't even browned at the edges.

As James walked to his classroom, he tried to make plans to show everyone his super speed. But he was so hungry all he could think about was food. It was weird still being hungry after that huge breakfast.

It was like the worms in his arms and legs were eating everything he ate. James started chewing his nails, but they weren't very filling.

He was so desperate that finally he got Theresa White to sell him some of her candy. It cost him a dollar just for one little Slurp Bar. But it kept him alive until ten o'clock, when he was so hungry he was feeling dizzy.

"Are you all right?" asked Simon Jones, his best friend.

James shrugged. "I got kidnapped by aliens last night and they gave me super speed," he explained.

"Oh," said Simon. "That's nice."

"I guess," said James. "But I'm really hungry," he added.

"Silence!" snapped Mrs. Sharply.

Mrs. Sharply was thin and spiky, and she was the nastiest teacher in the school. She was probably the nastiest teacher in the whole world.

She hated everybody, especially children. She always made the class work in silence for hours and hours.

James put his head in his hands. He was suddenly so weak with hunger that he couldn't hold his head up any longer.

"I don't think James is feeling very well," Simon said.

Mrs. Sharply gave James a mean look through her glasses. "Well, go to the nurse," she said, waving him away. "Don't breathe your germs around here!"

The school nurse had a very kind smile, so James told her all about the aliens. She asked him if he thought he needed something to eat.

"Yes," said James, who was feeling so empty he was beginning to worry that his pants might fall down.

So she gave him four cookies from the staff-room. He promised not to tell anybody in case she got into trouble. Then he went back to class.

James got through the next hour by chewing the end of his pencil and biting his nails until his fingers were sore.

At recess, instead of playing soccer, he had to go around begging for food.

He stuffed himself solid with two Crunchoes, three Yummies, four CaloriBars, five Licksy Biscuits, and a large bag of Jelly Eels.

Simon watched him. "It's going to cost a lot of money for you to have super speed," he said. He was helping by unwrapping the candy so James could eat it faster. "And you're going to get cavities."

James stuffed the last chocolate bar into his mouth and nodded. He felt really sick, but after eating all the candy he thought he could make it to lunchtime without turning into a skeleton.

Chapter 4

James didn't get a chance to use his super speed until lunchtime because of Mrs. Sharply.

Mrs. Sharply was dangerous. Her eyes were so cold and mean that she could freeze you all the way from the other side of the classroom.

She could make people cry just by raising her eyebrows. If anyone made a noise, she made everybody stay inside during recess.

As soon as the lunch bell rang, James rushed to the cafeteria at super speed to eat five helpings of everything.

The cafeteria had that funny smell, too, but all the food was great.

James went outside after he ate. He was really full, but he didn't care because this was the moment he'd been waiting for. Now James could show everybody that he was the best soccer player in the world.

He was, too. It was wonderful. He could run rings around people until they were dizzy. He could zoom by and take the ball, even from big boys like Chunky Baxter.

Once James got the ball, no one could catch him.

It was fantastic! He scored ten goals.

"Hey," said Chunky Baxter. "How come you're so good all of a sudden?"

Chunky Baxter was big. Really big. James looked up at him and wondered if scoring ten goals against Chunky had been the best thing to do.

"It's because he was kidnapped by aliens who gave him super speed," explained Simon.

"Oh," said Chunky. "That explains it." He began to walk off, but then he stopped.

"I've never beat up anyone who's been kidnapped by aliens," he said.

James began to back away.

"Come here," said Chunky Baxter calmly.

People didn't bother to run away from Chunky Baxter, because his legs could go really fast.

James was just about to give up, when he remembered his super speed.

He ran like a rocket. It was incredible!

He could run so fast that by the time Chunky Baxter figured out what was happening, James had been around the playground twice.

Everything looked blurry. It was almost like flying, and the only bad thing was that the burning smell had come back.

And at that moment, his socks burst into flames.

James yelped and jumped in the air.

All the girls screamed, but Simon shouted, "The pond, James! The pond!"

James zipped across the playground at super super speed and jumped right in.

The pond was freezing.

James stood there cooling off his ankles, with the mud slowly covering his shoes. What if there hadn't been a pond?

"What's going on?" asked Mrs. Sharply. She looked up from where she was sitting on a bench, reading her book.

When Simon tried to explain about the aliens, he was sent to stand in the hallway. James had to spend the rest of recess sitting at his desk with his arms folded.

James didn't mind.

He was afraid to move in case he burst into flames again.

"Are you all right?" Simon asked after the bell rang. He brought James a bag of chips.

James had been scared stiff, soaked through, and now he was starving again.

"I'm going to have to get the aliens to take away my super speed," he said sadly.

"Maybe they'll give you something better, instead," said Simon. "Maybe they'll turn you into a monster and then you can eat Mrs. Sharply."

"I'd rather eat mold," James said.

"Well, you could just scare her, then," Simon suggested. "Just so her hair stands up and her eyes fall out and she runs screaming out of school and no one ever sees her again."

James suddenly felt much happier.

His super speed had got him into a lot of trouble.

But maybe, if he thought and thought, he'd be able to figure out something to do about Mrs. Sharply.

Just then, she appeared in the classroom, stared at Simon and James with lizard eyes, and sent them to stand in corners for talking.

That gave James a chance to make some new plans.

He was going to use his super speed one last time, before he was finished with it forever.

Chapter 5

Mrs. Sharply drove a fancy white car. Mr. Sharply, who was bald and thin and always looked scared, had won the lottery the year before. Mrs. Sharply had bought herself a big car and a fur coat.

She made poor Mr. Sharply stay at home and do the housework, except for when she needed him to carry things. Everybody felt sorry for him.

James waited by the school gates for a long time before he saw Mrs. Sharply.

James waved to her as she drove the poor car, tires screaming, around the corner.

She scowled at James but that didn't spoil his plan.

He ran along at super speed until he got to the end of the road. Then he stood by the curb and waved again. She looked at him twice, that time.

The third time he waved to her, next to the drug store, she looked confused. James sped up again.

Some men were fixing the road nearby. There were huge steaming buckets of tar. The men mixed the tar, and tipped the buckets onto the ground.

Then steamrollers squashed the gunk into sleek blackness.

The workmen were eating lunch.

They didn't notice James when he ran out in front of a tar bucket and waved at the fancy white car that was coming down the road.

This time Mrs. Sharply's face turned white, as if she'd seen a ghost. She screamed so loud that James could see right down her throat.

Then she pointed the car at him and sped up. If James hadn't been super-fast she might have gotten him, but he managed to zip out of the way.

Mrs. Sharply's car hit the huge bucket with the biggest crunch James had ever heard. The bucket rocked, swung around, and crashed over, splattering black tar all over the road.

The car went up on its back wheels, almost hit the steamroller, and ended up across the road with its hood half open.

It took Mrs. Sharply a little while to get out of the car. She had to climb out through the trunk because the locks were jammed. She got tar all over her skirt.

James hung around to hear what the workmen had to say.

They were really rude. Mrs. Sharply tried to move in close to zap their insides with a blast of her evil stare. But her heels were stuck in the new road surface.

She had to go home in her bare feet.

But then Mrs. Sharply saw James through the bush. She looked so mean that his bones turned to jelly. He took off, and he didn't stop running till he got home and slammed the door behind him.

Tina sniffed at him as he stood panting in the hall. "Mom!" she called. "James has been smoking! He stinks!"

Mom hurried in.

"You haven't, have you?" she asked, sniffing him. "Don't you dare start smoking, James!"

"No," said James. "I haven't been smoking. Mom, what's for dinner? I'm so hungry!"

Tina pointed a long, accusing fingernail at him. "All his clothes are burned," she said. "Look at his jeans."

James looked down at his clothes.

The hems of his jeans were brown, and so was the front of his shirt.

Mom looked at him. "How did that happen?"

James tried to think of something to say, but he was so hungry all he could think of was food. Golden chicken strips and French fries. "I was watching the construction crew melt the tar onto the road," he said.

"That's stupid," said Tina, tossing back her purple hair. "You're always getting in people's way."

"Mrs. Sharply drove into a big bucket of tar," said James, suddenly happy.

"It went all over her car, and when she got out, her shoes got stuck in it."

Tina was grinning, too.

Mom sighed.

"We'll just have to hope the burn marks wash out," she said. "But you stay away from fire in the future, James. It's not safe!"

Super speed had been pretty fun, some of the time, but James was glad he was getting it taken away.

"Don't worry, Mom," he said, as he made his way to the kitchen.

He'd have a big meal, and then he'd sit down in front of the TV to wait for the giant hand.

"It won't happen again," he said.

* * *

"What was wrong with it?" asked Pockle, sounding offended, as James sat up on the shiny floor of the spaceship.

"It made me hungry," said James, "and my clothes caught on fire."

"We could give you fireproof fur," Pockle said. "It will work up to a thousand miles per hour."

"No, thanks," said James.

Pockle shook his head. "Fine. We'll take it away," he said. "What should we try next? Horns? Would poison glands come in useful, do you think?"

James shuddered. "No, thanks."

Pockle sighed. "Goodness knows what the rest of you humans are like," he said, "if you're the best there is."

"Am I really the best?" asked James. "The best in the whole world? Why?"

"Because you're young, for one thing. Adults are hopeless. Once they know they're in a spaceship they just cry. You're absolutely average in every way. Now, how would you like a small trunk?" asked Pockle. He squinted down at his own.

"Maybe one like mine. It's good for getting that last bit of milkshake out of the glass, and it works great, just like a vacuum cleaner."

"No way," said James.

A beeping noise sounded through all the ticking and whirrings of the ship.

"We're almost out of range," said Trada.

"Well, we'd better get going," said Pockle. "So what will you have improved, young human?"

"I don't know," said James. "I've been thinking about it all day, but I can't decide. I mean, I thought super speed would be a good idea, and look at all the disasters it caused. You should have picked someone smarter. Someone who would know what to choose."

Pockle suddenly smiled. "Let's give you some super brains, then," he said. "Just what you need. Now, super brains are a little different from super speed. For one thing, they'll take effect almost as soon as you get home."

"So I'll be really smart?" asked James.

"Oh yes, very smart. Your brains are going to be stuffed full of smartness. Are we ready, Miss Trada?" Pockle asked.

"Yeah. Well, I think I've pressed the right button," she said.

"Let's go, then," said Pockle.

James suddenly realized what was going to happen. Aliens were about to start messing around with his brain. He opened his mouth to tell them to stop, but it was too late.

Chapter 6

James woke up in his armchair. He felt as if his head was full of electric sponges. He sat up carefully.

"You're turning into a real sleepyhead, James," said Mom, who was sitting knitting in front of the news. "This is the second time I've found you asleep in front of the TV. You're not sick, are you?"

James blinked and tried to figure out why he was feeling so weird.

Super brains?

"I'm all right," he said. But he wasn't sure if it was true.

"Good. Your sweater's almost done!" Mom said.

The electric sponges in his head started cooking like sausages, and then James felt his hand picking up Mom's knitting pattern. He understood it. It was weird.

Before he knew what was happening, the sponges were figuring out the math problems. And here was the answer.

"You have 98 more rows to knit," he heard himself say. "That means that you completed 33.75 percent of the back of the sweater."

Mom stared at him. "I did?" she asked James.

His brain was now working out something called a standard deviation, and he didn't know how to stop it.

It was horrible! It was like having worms in his brain, and they kept wiggling and wriggling around.

He staggered off to bed.

***

At school the next day, his brain figured out how many tiles there were in the school hall, and then estimated the number of hairs left on Mr. Halford's head.

"You all right?" asked Simon.

James shook his head. "Those aliens gave me super brains," he said. "They made me really smart."

"Oh," said Simon. "What's it like?"

"Awful!" cried James. He hadn't slept the night before because his brain had been figuring out stupid things like the average time it took his family to use up a toilet paper roll. "It's like having dancing worms in your head."

"Oh," said Simon.

Mrs. Sharply was in a particularly mean mood that morning because her car was being fixed and she'd had to take the bus.

She made up a mean quiz for the class. They had to add up all the numbers from one to 100.

The class sighed, but James did the problem before he even knew it.

It was easy. The numbers from one to 100 could be made into forty-nine pairs. One and 99, two and 98, and so on. Each pair added up to 100. Leftover were the numbers 50 and 100. So that made 5,050.

He wrote it down and then leaned back to take a nap. But his brain didn't want to sleep. It kept thinking about the number of threads in the carpet.

"James Hunter!" snapped a voice. James quickly opened his eyes.

"Why aren't you doing your work?" demanded Mrs. Sharply.

"I finished it," he said. The class gasped.

"Some aliens have given him super brains," said Simon helpfully.

This upset Mrs. Sharply, so she made James clean the supply closet. Being smart didn't help that at all.

"I can't stand it!" exclaimed James at lunch. "My brain keeps thinking about boring stuff. It's like living with a million sisters!" Simon turned pale at the thought.

Mrs. Platt, the nicest lunch lady, noticed James's tired look and asked him if he'd like to lie down.

"He's not sick," explained Simon. "He was kidnapped by aliens and they gave him super brains. He feels like he has worms dancing in his head."

"Oh dear," said Mrs. Platt calmly. "These aliens get everywhere, nowadays," she said. "Why don't you go play? It'll take your mind off it."

James tried, but it didn't work.

The ticking in his head meant he couldn't think about the game.

"You're playing really badly today," said Chunky Baxter.

"I know," said James sadly. "It's my super brains. I'm too smart, and that doesn't leave any room for soccer."

"Oh," said Chunky. "Well, I'm glad I'm stupid, then."

Some kids from their class gathered around.

"Hey, James!" said Harry. "What's 302.5 divided by 6.2?"

Fizz-fizz-fizz-ting!

"48.790322," said James sadly.

Harry checked it on his watch calculator. "Wow!" he said.

James put his hands over his ears. "Don't ask me any more," he said. "It makes my head feel horrible."

"I'm going to ask him a square root," said Veronica. "That's the most difficult kind of problem. James, what's the square root of 7.1?"

James didn't want to answer, but his brain had worked it out and the answer was wiggling out his tongue.

"2.6645825," he gulped.

"Right!" said Harry, poking at his watch. "James knows everything!"

"I don't, I don't," said James. "I can just figure stuff out."

People began to look thoughtful.

"Could you figure out how to get rid of Mrs. Sharply?" asked Simon.

James clamped his mouth shut.

The answer was rising up in his brain like a huge burp.

"A bomb would do it," he said, unable to stop the words.

"Wow," said Harry. "Do you know how to make one?"

And James did. It was terrible.

"I do!" he squeaked. "Everything we need is in the janitor's closet!"

Everyone was suddenly grinning, except Veronica. "That's an awful idea," she said. "Someone might get hurt."

"Yes," said James. "And we'd get put in prison forever, until we were as old as Mr. Halford is."

Everyone stopped grinning.

"Why is there always some stupid problem?" asked Harry.

"Why can't we have a nice teacher?" asked Simon, sighing.

James felt the worms in his brain fizzing and squirming again. They did wild cartwheels. James clenched his teeth, but his thoughts were bursting out of him.

"We can!" he squeaked. "We can give her a pill to erase all of her meanness!"

People looked at each other.

"How would we make it?" asked Simon.

A huge list started coming out of James's mouth.

"Three oak leaves, some belly-button lint, a piece of chalk, a wet booger, a pound of potato peelings."

His mouth finally stopped talking, and there was silence.

Then a squishing sound.

"Well, I've got the booger," said Chunky Baxter.

James made the pill in less than one minute.

Harry bought a Slurp Bar from Theresa, dug out some of the cream, and put the pill inside.

It was easy to get Mrs. Sharply to eat it.

As soon as they got back to the classroom, Harry let her see it, and she grabbed it right away.

She popped it in her mouth.

Right away Mrs. Sharply turned green. "I hope she doesn't puke," whispered Simon.

Then Mrs. Sharply turned blue, then white, and then, incredibly, she smiled. "Oh, what wonderful chocolate," she said.

"And just look at all your sweet little faces! I feel so happy to be here with you special children. Sweet Simon, and perfect Harry."

She stopped speaking and swayed a little. Then she fell over.

Veronica knew what to do because her mom was a nurse. She put her fingers on Mrs. Sharply's bony wrist.

"Mrs. Sharply's heart's not beating," Veronica reported.

"Is that bad?" asked Chunky.

"Well," said Simon. "It does mean she's dead."

"Could be worse, then," said Harry.

But James felt his super brains squirming by his left ear.

They were figuring out what was going to happen.

"People will say it's all our fault," he said. "They'll say she was poisoned."

"But nothing we gave her was poisonous," pointed out Simon. "It shouldn't have killed her."

But James had figured that out, too. "She was so horrible that with all the mean stuff gone there's nothing left. Her heart's just an empty shell."

"I don't want to go to prison!" wailed Veronica. "It's not fair!"

James felt his brains working.

He thought so hard that the worms in his brain turned into flies and buzzed around his skull until his teeth felt loose. There was only one way out of this.

"I'm going to have to make an antidote," he said.

"What's an antidote?" Chunky asked.

James sighed. Of course he knew the answer. "It's something that stops the pill from working." He quickly mixed up some leftover ingredients with spit and threw the pill into Mrs. Sharply's mouth.

Mrs. Sharply sat up at once. "What are you all doing out of your seats?" she snapped.

"I just saved your life," said James.

"Nonsense," said Mrs. Sharply. "You can't possibly think I'm stupid enough to believe that, James Hunter."

James tried to keep his mouth shut, but the answer was pushing at his eardrums.

"Yes, I can!" he heard himself say, even though his insides were shaking with horror. "And you're mean, too!"

James wondered if the easiest thing might be to run away.

Mrs. Sharply put her face down to his.

"Never forget that you are in my power, James Hunter," she hissed.

Then she made James stand on a chair at the front of the classroom all afternoon and do math on the whiteboard.

It wasn't fair, thought James angrily.

His super brains ran around inside his head like crazy hamsters. His hand wrote out rows and rows of stuff he couldn't understand.

He just wanted to go home.

"What's all this?" demanded Mrs. Sharply, later.

"It's how to build a time machine," said James. He was shocked.

"Erase it right now!" screamed Mrs. Sharply.

"I hope your dancing worms get better," said Simon seriously, as they were putting their coats on.

"They will," said James. "I'm having them taken out tonight."

He could hardly wait.

Chapter 7

James usually watched cartoons after school, but that day his brain made him switch to the history channel.

James had one hamburger, 156 beans, and 25 French fries for dinner.

"Mom!" said Tina. "Tell James to stop playing with his food!"

"What are you doing?" asked Mom.

James turned red. He put down his ruler. "Measuring how much milk is in my glass," he said.

After dinner, he sat down to watch TV again. Luckily, Mom and Tina were looking through a clothes catalog, and Dad was delivering a truckload of beans, so he had the room to himself.

His super brains were still chattering. They counted the number of flowers on the wallpaper, and how far his French fries would reach, added end to end. The answer was two hundred inches.

Then, just as he was about to try tearing his head off, the TV turned fuzzy and a bony hand appeared on the screen.

James saw the glow of Pockle's spaceship with relief.

Pockle was looking extra slimy. "So how did the super brains go?" he asked.

"Terrible," growled James. "It's like having dancing worms in my head. Take it away."

"Something else, then?" said Pockle, with a sigh. "Any ideas?"

James's super brains had thought of lots of ideas. His favorite was being turned into Mr. Halford so he could fire Mrs. Sharply. That would be fun, but Mom would notice the difference at breakfast the next day.

"Look, I think the best thing would be if you put me back to normal and just let me go home," James said.

Pockle walked around in a small circle.

"One more try," he said. "Just one more, and if that doesn't work out we'll give up on this stupid planet and go somewhere else, all right?"

James thought about it. One last try.

Maybe he could handle one more try, as long as he knew it really was going to be the last.

"Okay," he said slowly. He thought about it carefully. "I guess flying would be fun," he said.

"Certainly," said Pockle, rubbing his claws together. "Easy. We'll just hollow out your bones, and move your ribs."

"Oh no," said James quickly. "No way. You're not messing with my bones."

But what should he have? Something really cool. Super what? Super vision? Super hearing? Super strength?

Super strength?

Then he'd be the strongest person in the school. The strongest person in the world, probably.

His class had liked his super speed and super brains. They would love it if he had super strength. Maybe if he was super strong, Mrs. Sharply wouldn't be so scary.

"Super strength?" he suggested.

Trada stopped twisting foil into her hair and pulled down the instruction book.

This time, James decided, he'd be really careful. He'd hardly use his super strength at all. He'd just try it out once or twice to see what happened.

Trada licked a pink claw, turned a page, and typed in a whole bunch of stuff very quickly.

And then James changed his mind. He didn't want to be super.

Being super just gave you super-sized problems. Why hadn't his super brains figured that out before?

He opened his mouth to tell her to stop!

But he was too late.

* * *

James woke up the next morning and opened his eyes.

His super brains must have really tired him out, because even though the dancing worms had shut up he was feeling heavy and tired.

He had an awful feeling that today was going to be a really bad day.

When he was brushing his teeth his toothbrush broke. He showed his mom.

"It broke," he said.

Mom looked at the toothbrush.

"All by itself?"

"Yes," said James, sighing. It had been a really cool purple toothbrush.

"Well, that's the first time I've ever heard of such a thing happening, James. Are you sure you weren't doing something silly with it?"

"Of course I wasn't!" James said.

Mom sighed. "Well, I don't have time to talk about it now, James. I'm late. Make sure you slam the door when you leave, okay? It hasn't been closing right."

James stomped downstairs, picked up his backpack, and let himself out. He slammed the front door.

The door handle came off in his hand.

He stared at it, even more angry and surprised than before. Now the door handle had fallen to pieces.

Why was everything breaking apart around him? And then he realized.

Aliens, he thought. Super strength.

Oh no!

James kicked the broken door handle.

It zoomed up and crashed right through the wood of the door.

James thought about trying to put it all back together, but the door had a big jagged hole in it and there was nothing he could do.

James opened the garden gate very carefully, and walked slowly up the road.

That morning James's class started with Language Arts. His pencil point broke right away.

He sharpened it, but even though he was really careful it snapped again after only a couple of words. James was so strong it was scary.

He went up to the front of the classroom again and sharpened his broken pencil again.

He got a mean stare from Mrs. Sharply again, and went back to his seat.

Snap!

"What's up?" asked Simon, in the smallest possible whisper.

James held up his broken pencil.

"I'm super strong," he whispered back.

Simon gave a silent whistle and handed over a pencil sharpener.

"Thanks," said James.

He grabbed it, and crushed it into a thousand pieces between his fingers.

Everyone in the class heard the crunch.

A tiny whisper ran around the room. "He's super strong!"

The class was suddenly alive with hope.

James was super strong.

Maybe today they could somehow get back at Mrs. Sharply.

James kept working very gently so he would not break the point of his pencil again.

He wondered what to do.

Chapter 8

Chunky Baxter couldn't see what the problem was. "Pull her head off," he said.

James shook his head. "I'm not touching her," he said.

Everybody thought hard.

"You could scare her so much that she runs away and falls over a cliff," suggested Harry.

"How?" James asked.

"Go crazy. Tear up her desk," Harry replied, smiling.

"Oh, right," said James. "What would Mr. Halford say?"

"He won't mind," said Harry. "He hates Mrs. Sharply as much as we do. It's only a desk. Go on, James! Do it!"

Everyone else was nodding.

"Okay, okay," said James. "I'll think about it."

Super strength was not fun. James had to be really careful in case he touched someone and broke their bones. People kept coming up to him and whispering that he should do something. He didn't know what to do.

Simon was the only one who understood. "Later," he kept telling everyone. "He's going to do it later. Leave him alone."

By lunch time, people were getting restless. "You're lying," someone said in the playground. "You couldn't peel a banana."

Simon handed James his empty soda can. James squeezed it down to the size of an acorn and flicked it at a garage. The garage's walls fell down and the roof caved in.

They all found themselves staring at the janitor, who was sitting on a paint can with a doughnut halfway to his mouth.

Everyone stood perfectly still, open-mouthed, until the echoes had died away.

No one bothered James after that.

They played baseball that afternoon. James was the first to be picked.

Everyone on his team ran out onto the field smirking, and the others trudged and sulked.

James missed the ball completely on his first two tries, but the third time he hit it.

The ball went up like a missile. It went across the playing field, over the bushes, and right over the row of houses next to the school.

The class watched in awe as it hit a chimney, bounced back, whizzed over their heads, flew off the jungle gym, and landed with a thud in the bushes by the school entrance.

"Wow!" said the class.

"Tsk!" said Mrs. Sharply. "You horrible boy. How could you be so careless with school property? You will sit out the games for the rest of the year. Now, go with Veronica and find that ball. And hurry up!"

James walked slowly across the playing field and Veronica skipped along beside him. "Ooh," she said, "you are strong, James. Hey, James!"

"What?"

"Don't you think we should hold hands if we're going near the highway?" asked Veronica sweetly.

James sighed.

He thought it was going to take all afternoon to find the ball (that is, if it hadn't bounced up again and gone into orbit).

But it wasn't long before Veronica bounced up to him.

"Look, I found it," she said. "And I was careful not to walk on the flower bed. Come on, James. Back to school!"

James followed her slowly.

It was hard to keep up with her because his muscles were made of iron or something, and they weighed him down.

"Come on, James!"

James turned the corner by the pond, but then he was suddenly too tired to go any further.

He leaned against a tree to get his breath back.

And it fell over.

James felt the ground moving under his feet, and then the whole tree tipped and fell through the bushes.

To make things even worse, it got tangled up in the wires of a telephone pole.

It pulled out the pole, too, and the whole thing crashed down onto the road.

"Oh no!" Veronica shouted.

In the big hole in the ground where the telephone pole had been there were layers of thick cables, and they were all fizzing and spitting as if lots of electricity was leaking out.

Across the road an alarm went off. All the lights had gone out in the stores. There were no lights in the school, either.

Even the street light on the other side of the hill had gone out.

Oh no! thought James. He turned around very carefully and went back to his class.

Since the whole school had no electricity, everyone had to sit in the gym for the longest assembly ever. It was torture.

When school was over, James ran home.

He couldn't wait to have his super strength taken away.

He'd forgotten all about the damage to the front door. The hole in it looked even bigger than before.

No matter what, he wasn't getting any more super things from the aliens.

James was searching very carefully in his pocket for his key when he realized he could hear something.

A rustling noise was coming from inside the house. He listened carefully. There was no doubt about it.

Burglars!

All of a sudden his heart was beating very fast.

It's all right, he thought. I'm strong. I can handle a burglar.

He opened the door very gently and quietly. He listened closely.

There was someone in the house.

 Chapter 9

James took a cautious step into the hall. If he could catch a burglar he might get his name in the paper. He might even get a medal.

James took another step forward, and then he gulped. There was a pair of big black boots sticking out of the storage space under the stairs.

It was lucky James was super strong. He'd have to be careful not to hurt the burglar too much.

What James would do was yank the burglar out by the legs. Then he'd sit on the burglar until he gave back everything he'd stolen.

Then James would call the police, and police cars would come screeching up. It would be awesome.

James tiptoed forward very quietly. Then he grabbed the burglar's ankles and pulled hard. It worked like a charm. The burglar shot out backwards, and James sat down gently on top of him.

And all the burglar said was "Ooomph!" and lay still with his nose squashed into the carpet.

When the burglar began to move James said, "You keep still or I'll break your arms off!" in a deep, growly voice.

The burglar forced its head sideways and spat out pieces of carpet fluff. "Yuck! Yuck!" it said.

James blinked and looked at the burglar more closely.

It had purple hair. It had long red fingernails. It had a tattoo on its neck.

"Get off me!" shouted Tina.

Getting off Tina wasn't safe. But then neither was sitting on her until Mom came home.

James got up and ran to the door of the living room.

Tina heaved herself to her feet.

"I thought you were a burglar," said James sadly.

Tina pushed back her hair. "That really hurt," she said.

"I'm sorry, Tina," said James. He really, really was. "But your head was in the storage space!"

Tina brushed fluff off her black sweater.

"I was fixing a fuse!" she snapped. "The electricity's off."

"That was an accident," said James.

Tina's black eyes widened. She pointed a finger at James, and then she let out a howl. "You broke one of my nails!"

James turned and ran.

He dived into the living room and slammed the door just as Tina hit it. The handle came off in his hand.

There was a loud thud and the door rattled, but James was rushing to turn on the TV.

Hurry up, Pockle, he thought. Hurry up!

But nothing happened. Nothing at all. The TV screen stayed dead and black. Of course it wasn't working. James had just turned off the whole town's electricity.

A figure appeared outside the open window. It was Tina.

She would climb in through the window. She'd pull his hair, and poke him with her sharp nails (the ones he hadn't broken).

James wouldn't be able to do anything back to her in case she fell to pieces.

"I couldn't help it," he said. "I mean it."

Tina kept on coming.

"Help!" screamed James, though there was no one to hear him.

Tina's massive hand was pulling open the window.

"Pockle!" yelled James. "You got me into this mess! Pockle, help!"

"Who's Pockle?" asked Tina, carefully lifting her second leg through the window and jumping down to the floor.

"He's an alien. He keeps kidnapping me," said James. "Pockle!"

Tina snorted. "I wish he'd kept you."

"Don't hit me," pleaded James. "Look, I'll ask Pockle to improve you, too, if you want. I'll ask him to get rid of that tattoo on your neck."

Tina's hand went up to it. "It's a great tattoo," she said.

"Yeah," said James, "but think how nice it would be if it wasn't there. Pockle could do that."

Tina looked at him. "You must be crazy," she said, but there was a little bit of doubt in her voice.

The TV made a sudden crackling noise and swirls began to wave across the screen.

"Pockle!" called James. "Pockle, come and get me!"

"Where does he take you?" asked Tina.

"Up to his spaceship. Pockle!"

The screen turned soapy green.

James braced himself for the horrible feeling of the bony hand grabbing him.

Tina suddenly jumped at him and threw her arms around his neck.

"Get off me!" he said.

But James was already miles above the town. He could see it, all green and blotchy beneath him. And here were the clouds, bashing him wetly in the face.

Tina was with him. Her mouth was wide open, but they were going so fast that her screams were being left far behind them.

Here was the darkness of space, and the glow of Pockle's spaceship, and then they were there.

Chapter 10

Pockle peered at them. "Oh my," he said. "What's this?"

"It's a sister," said James. "She grabbed me right before you did."

Tina's eyes were bulging out. "It's a space monster," she said. "Help!"

"Interesting," said Pockle. "Who do you think will hear you?"

"No one, really," explained James. "She's just sort of hoping."

"Ah! Well, never mind. How is your super strength, young man?"

James frowned. "It's horrible. Really horrible. I hate it. Everything I touch breaks in pieces. I already smashed up half of our house."

"You humans really are the most difficult creatures," Pockle said, sighing.

"Sorry," said James, "but that's how we are. In fact, I've decided I'm perfectly fine as I am, thank you very much."

Trada looked up from painting her nostrils. "Funny," she said. "That's what the whales said."

Pockle lifted himself onto his stool.

"Oh well," he said sadly. "That's another three thousand years of my life down the drain. I thought that pointing out how badly designed humans are would help them, but it seems there's nothing we can do. Head toward home, Miss Trada."

Tina pushed herself up on one elbow. She stopped crying.

"You could give me stronger nails," she suggested. "My fake ones are terrible. They're costing me a fortune."

"No, don't, Tina," said James. "You'd probably have to cut them off with a chainsaw or something."

"It'd be better than having bitten nails like yours!" she said.

"Yeah, but what if you caught one on something? You'd probably tear your finger off."

Tina shivered at the thought, but Pockle's ears had pricked up.

"Are you saying that it's wrong for your species to eat your nails?" he said. "Well then. How about if I made them taste terrible?"

James tried to think of a reason why not. He couldn't.

"Could you take off my tattoo, too?" asked Tina.

"Your tattoo?" echoed Trada. "But it's so cool."

"Yeah," Tina said. "It is. But it looks a little weird when I wear a swimsuit."

A buzzer began to beep.

"We need to send you back," said Pockle. He clapped his hands together. "Anything else we can do for you while we're here?"

"No," said James.

"Are you sure?"

"Well, you could fix all the things my super strength broke," said James.

"No problem," said Pockle. "I'll send the hand down now. Anything else?"

James thought. "You couldn't do something about Mrs. Sharply, could you?" he asked.

"Well, I suppose we could take her home with us," Pockle suggested.

James was shocked. His jaw dropped. Take Mrs. Sharply away? To another planet?

"What would you do with her?" asked Tina in an awestruck voice.

"Oh, freeze her, and make a working model of her to put in our museum. And then once we did that we'd pop her back down on Earth," said Pockle.

James had an awful feeling, but he couldn't say anything.

"How long would she be gone?" asked Tina, sounding excited.

"Oh, not more than ten thousand years, at the most. That would be all right, wouldn't it? I mean, no one would miss her, would they?"

James thought.

Who would miss Mrs. Sharply? Not anyone in the school. Not poor Mr. Sharply.

James slowly shook his head. "Our class watches the news right away in the morning," he said slowly.

"All right, we'll pick her up then. Oh, I do feel better knowing we're going to do something useful. It's been nice knowing you. Are you ready?" Pockle asked.

James sat down on the floor. He was definitely ready.

* * *

"Well, aren't you two a bundle of energy!" Someone was talking. James took a deep breath and struggled to open his eyes. He sat up.

Tina was on the couch looking dazed, and Dad was smiling at them.

"What happened to the spaceship?" asked Tina.

Dad chuckled.

"I've always thought you lived on another planet, Tina, but I never knew you actually had a spaceship," he said. "Does it have little green men on it who go beep beep?"

Tina blushed.

"I dreamed a hand came out of the TV and took James and me up to a spaceship," she said. "And there were two aliens on it named Pockle and —"

"Trada," said James.

"Yeah," said Tina. "Hey, how did you know that?"

"I was on the spaceship!" said James.

Dad laughed and wandered out to the kitchen.

Tina was staring at James.

She got up and went over to the mirror. She turned her head around to try to see the back of her neck.

"It's gone," said James. Then he had another thought.

He scanned his hands carefully, searching for a finger with a little bit of bitable nail on it.

"Yuck!" The taste of it was just revolting. It tasted like broccoli and earwax. It was so bad that James had to run to the sink to rinse his mouth out.

Tina caught him as he was hunting through the fridge for something to take the taste away. "You tell anyone I was on that spaceship," she said, waving a finger in his face, "and you're in big trouble. So just forget it and pretend to be normal."

That wasn't going to be hard, because he was back to normal. No more bursting into flames, no more dancing worms keeping him awake, no more being afraid to hit Tina in case she fell to pieces.

He was grinning from ear to ear.

"It's great, isn't it?" he asked.

Chapter 11

When James got to school the next day everyone wanted to know what new super power he had.

"I'm just ordinary, now," he said. "I'm back to normal, except that my nails taste like broccoli and earwax. The aliens are going home today."

Everyone was disappointed, and James had to promise to let them taste his nail clippings once his nails had grown.

"Too bad you didn't get to do anything to Mrs. Sharply," Harry said.

James shrugged and kept quiet.

The first thing Mrs. Sharply did in class that morning was switch on the television. Then she stared at everyone with a frown and sat down.

Everyone sighed and turned to watch the screen.

Two minutes into the program, a message appeared:

> MRS. SHARPLY IS ABOUT TO
> BE KIDNAPPED BY ALIENS

Simon looked at James. "What? Mrs. Sharply's getting superpowers?" he exclaimed, horrified.

"Simon Jones, stop talking!" snapped Mrs. Sharply.

The television turned a swirly green, and a bony hand formed in the depths of the screen.

"I don't know who's been playing with the TV," Mrs. Sharply went on, "but no recess until I find out!"

You could see all the bones in the bony hand, now.

"Aliens!" screamed Veronica. "They're coming to get you!"

"Veronica, don't be silly," said Mrs. Sharply. "Everyone knows there are no such things as — ooooooooooomph!"

The whole class sat, silent with wonder.

"Um, I'm looking for Mrs. Sharply," said a voice behind them.

It was poor Mr. Sharply, looking even thinner and more worried than usual. He was carrying a huge pile of books.

"Some aliens have just kidnapped her," explained Simon, into the silence.

Mr. Sharply blinked. "Oh. Why?"

James couldn't stop smiling. "They're going to freeze her and make a model of her for their museum," he said happily.

"And she isn't going to be coming back for ten thousand years," he added.

Mr. Sharply stared at him as if he could hardly believe it.

"Ten thousand years?" he whispered.

James suddenly realized what a shock this must be.

Whoops.

"Ten thousand years?" Mr. Sharply asked again. "Ten thousand?"

Everyone in the class had their mouths wide open.

Then Mr. Sharply suddenly threw out his arms and fifty books sailed flapping through the air.

"Ten thousand years!" shouted Mr. Sharply at the top of his voice.

"Yippee!"

Mr. Halford came into the room to see what all the noise was about.

As far as he could tell, it was because Mrs. Sharply had resigned.

And that was such good news that he went back to his study and shouted "Yippee!"

Nobody heard him.

Outside in the playground Chunky Baxter was running around hooting like a baboon, and everyone else was jumping up and down with joy.

They were carrying James Hunter on their shoulders.

And they were all cheering.

About the Author

Sally Prue first started making up stories as a teenager, when she realized that designing someone else's adventures was almost as satisfying as having her own! At school, Sally was always fascinated by words and their histories. Sally and her husband live in England and have two daughters. She now works as a recorder and piano teacher and enjoys walking, painting, day-dreaming, reading, and gardening. She has two elderly guinea pigs.

Glossary

alien (AY-lee-uhn)—a creature from outer space

burglar (BURG-lur)—someone who breaks into a house or building in order to steal

concentrate (KON-suhn-trate)—to keep one's attention on something

genius (JEEN-yuhss)—someone who has a very great natural ability to think and create

maggot (MAG-uht)—the larva of a fly. A maggot looks like a small worm.

politics (POL-uh-tiks)—the management or activities of government

resign (re-ZINE)—to give up , to quit a job

sleek (SLEEK)—smooth and shiny

special effect (SPESH-uhl uh-FEKT)—a visual or sound effect added to a movie or television show

Discussion Questions

1. If you could be "redesigned," what would you want changed about yourself? What superpower would you choose? Discuss the reasons why.

2. The adults in this story all respond calmly when told that James was kidnapped by aliens. Why? Discuss your thinking.

3. Why did the aliens choose to help James (and this planet)?

4. How do you feel about what happens to Mrs. Sharply? What would you do to try to change or get rid of a teacher?

Writing Prompts

1. This story begins "One afternoon, James Hunter was kidnapped by aliens." Use this same sentence to start, but put your own name in place of James Hunter. Then write your own story.

2. How would you choose and put a "superpower" to good use? Write about it.

3. Trada, an alien, comments that James is ugly. ("No slime. Yuck!") Use the details in the story to draw a picture of how you think Trada looks.

Also Published by Stone Arch Books

Time and Again
Rob Childs

Becky and Chris discover a strange-looking watch with the power to travel back through time. Time travel is not as easy as they thought, especially when class troublemaker Luke decides to join them.

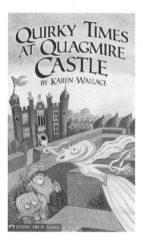

Quirky Times at Quagmire Castle
Karen Wallace

Jack and Emily have just been told that Quagmire Castle, their beloved, crumbling home, is going to be sold. Luckily, they meet their long-lost ghostly ancestors, and everything changes overnight.

Ghost School
S. Purkiss

Ghost kids have homework, just like human kids. As the Practical Haunting test looms in the near future, Spookers finds that the art of haunting is no easy task.

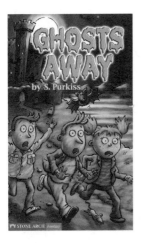

Ghosts Away
S. Purkiss

Young ghosts Spooker, Goof, and Holly are off to a remote Scottish castle to make an instructional video on haunting. Unfortunately, the castle turns out to be already haunted, and not just by other ghosts.

Internet Sites

Do you want to know more about subjects related to this book? Or are you interested in learning about other topics? Then check out FactHound, a fun, easy way to find Internet sites.

Our investigative staff has already sniffed out great sites for you!

Here's how to use FactHound:

1. Visit *www.facthound.com*

2. Select your grade level.

3. To learn more about subjects related to this book, type in the book's ISBN number: **1598891111**.

4. Click the **Fetch It** button.

FactHound will fetch the best Internet sites for you!